Rosie and the Robbers

Other titles in the bunch:

Baby Bear Comes Home
Big Dog and Little Dog Visit the Moon
Delilah Digs for Treasure   Dilly and the Goody-Goody
Horse in the House   I Don't Want to Say Yes!
Juggling with Jeremy   Keeping Secrets
Mabel and Max   Magnificent Mummies
Midnight at Memphis   Mouse Flute
The Nut Map   Owl in the House
Riff-Raff Rabbit   Rosie and the Robbers
Runaway Fred   Tom's Hats

First published in Great Britain 1998 by Mammoth
an imprint of Egmont Children's Books Limited
Michelin House, 81 Fulham Rd, London SW3 6RB
Published in hardback by Heinemann Library,
a division of Reed Educational and Professional Publishing Limited
by arrangement with Egmont Children's Books Limited.
Text copyright © Eric Houghton 1998
Illustrations copyright © Alex de Wolf 1998
The Author and Illustrator have asserted their moral rights
Paperback ISBN 0 7497 2867 1
Hardback ISBN 0 434 80087 2
10 9 8 7 6 5
A CIP catalogue record for this title is available from the British Library
Printed in Dubai

Rosie and the Robbers

Eric Houghton

Illustrated by Alex de Wolf

BLue Bananas

For Noah –

For Ned –

And for Andrew.

Once there was a princess called Rosie.
She had big feet and liked banana
sandwiches. She also liked steamrollers.
In fact, she collected them.

Her father, the King, was cross about the steamrollers. He didn't think a princess should go around driving steamrollers, or taking them to pieces and putting them together again in her bedroom.

One day the King

lost his temper.

He told Rosie:

'A princess should

not waste her time

with silly

steamrollers.

From now on,

I forbid you

to touch a

steamroller

again!'

Steamrollers are not silly!

Now it was Rosie's turn to get cross.
She stormed outside, threw her crown
on the ground and flattened it with
her fat steamroller.

9

Then she went to the palace kitchen
and made a huge pile of banana
sandwiches. She packed them into a
suitcase and hurried to the garage.

With tears in her eyes, she said goodbye to her other steamrollers – the short, tall and slim ones.

Rosie heaved her suitcase onto the fat steamroller. She drove straight through the palace wall into the Wild Wood where bears and other dangerous creatures lived.

In the darkest part of the Wild Wood
she met three robbers.

They looked very wicked.

Stop!

'What's in your suitcase? Is it
worth robbing?' they asked.

'I won't tell you unless you promise
to help me,' Rosie replied.

'All right, we promise,' the robbers said. 'Now, what's in your suitcase?'

'Tell you later,' said Rosie. 'First you must show me the way to your den.'

The way to the robbers' den was difficult and dangerous.

But Rosie was a skilful driver and

at last they reached the den.

The den was dark and dirty, with lots of spiders. Rosie loved it. She remembered her promise and showed the robbers what was in her suitcase.

Then she gave them a banana sandwich each and told them about her plan to rescue the steamrollers.

'Now, do any of you know how to drive a steamroller?' Rosie asked. The robbers shook their heads. Rosie sighed. She began to give them driving lessons.

Look out!

They weren't very good at it.

Now it was the robbers' turn to give

Rosie lessons. They lent her a

robber's mask,

 a robber's hat

and a cloak.

Next they showed

her how to look wicked.

Rosie was very good at it.

Then it was supper time, so Rosie

handed out more banana sandwiches.

After this, everyone went to sleep.

Rosie got up early the next morning

and woke the three robbers.

'We'll rescue my steamrollers now,'

she told them, 'before anyone at the

palace wakes up.'

The robbers groaned. Yawning and grumbling, they put on their robbers' outfits and ate breakfast. It was banana sandwiches.

After breakfast, Rosie climbed onto the
fat steamroller and started the engine.
'Hurry up,' she said. 'Remember your
lessons by watching me drive, and
don't touch any levers or play
with the toolbox!'

As the steamroller chuffed through the Wild Wood, the robbers saw a notice pinned to a tree. They read it and looked at Rosie.

MISSING PERSON
Princess Rosie.
She has big feet and likes banana sandwiches. If you find her, please return her to the King, who loves her very much
the King

'You could go back to him now,' the robbers said. But Rosie just scowled! 'He ordered me never to touch a steamroller again,' she said, 'so I'm never going back. Not ever.'

The steamroller chugged out of the wood and stopped outside the King's palace.

Rosie led the way, past the sleeping

sentries, to the garage.

She smiled when she saw
her three steamrollers
waiting to be rescued.

Can I drive
the short one?

This one's
mine!

'Remember the lessons I gave you,'
Rosie told the robbers. 'Start the
engines and follow me!'

Suddenly, over the puff-puffing of the

engines, came a dreadful noise . . .

It was the sound of fierce growling bears. They burst out of the Wild Wood and charged towards the palace! The sentries woke up at once and ran for their lives.

The King woke up too. He got dressed

and ran outside. 'Come back!' he shrieked

at the sentries. 'Come and save me first!'

The bears licked their lips and
bounded towards him. The King was
overcome with fright - and fainted.
He lay in a heap on the palace steps.

37

Rosie knew there was only one thing she could do. She drove her steamroller straight at the bears.

The three robbers tried to do the same.

Perhaps they should have had more

driving lessons . . .

Perhaps they should have looked where

they were going . . .

They missed the bears completely.

It was just bad luck they didn't

miss the palace

as well!

40

The bears had never heard such a horrible clashing, clanging and clattering. They fled back to the Wild Wood, howling in terror.

The King woke up from his faint.
He looked around and wondered
why he hadn't been eaten
by the bears.

Then he noticed the steamrollers
being driven by four masked robbers.
One of them had big feet and was
eating a banana sandwich.

'Rosie! You've come back

and saved me,' he cried.

'With help from my steamrollers!'

Rosie pointed out.

The King shook hands with the robbers.

'As a reward for saving me from the

bears,' he said, 'perhaps you'd

like to come and live

at the palace?'

'Yes please,'

said the robbers,

'as long as we

don't have to

drive any more

steamrollers.'

Rosie was glad her friends were staying
and got them to help her rebuild the
wrecked palace.

Perhaps that was why it ended up

looking different from before!

The King was so glad to have Rosie back that he didn't mind the changes – well, not much.

Rosie was glad to be home too. And from then on, the King let Rosie drive her steamrollers every day, while he went out birdwatching. Rosie always made him a picnic.

Don't forget your picnic, Dad!

Guess what she put in the sandwiches!